The equalizer looked certain when Simon was caught out of his goal and the ball was lobbed over his head. Everyone, it seemed, stopped and gave up to watch it bouncing towards the welcoming net – but not Andrew.

Hoping against hope, he simply kept chasing, desperate to reach the ball before it crossed the line. And he did – just! With less than a metre to spare, Andrew somehow managed to hook the ball away, tumbling head over heels into the goal himself instead . . .

It's September, and Andrew Weston is delighted to be picked to play in the school football team. He's determined to play as well as he can – and to help the team win every match! But first, both he and his younger brother Chris – a promising goalkeeper – have the chance to show what they can do in the annual Cubs six-a-side tournament.

THE BIG GAME

THE BIG GAME

ROB CHILDS

Illustrated by Tim Marwood

YOUNG CORGI BOOKS

THE BIG GAME
A YOUNG CORGI BOOK : 0 552 52804 8

First publication in Great Britain

PRINTING HISTORY
Young Corgi edition published 1994
Reprinted 1994, 1996

Text copyright © Rob Childs, 1994
Illustrations copyright © Tim Marwood, 1994
Cover illustration by Tony Kerins

This book is set in 14/18pt Century Schoolbook by
Phoenix Typesetting, Ilkley, West Yorkshire.

Young Corgi Books are published by Transworld Publishers Ltd,
61–63 Uxbridge Road, Ealing, London W5 5SA,
in Australia by Transworld Publishers (Australia) Pty Ltd,
15–25 Helles Avenue, Moorebank, NSW 2170,
and in New Zealand by Transworld Publishers (NZ) Ltd,
3 William Pickering Drive, Albany, Auckland.

Printed and bound in Great Britain by
Cox & Wyman Ltd, Reading, Berkshire.

*For all young footballers – keep play-ing and enjoying your soccer . . . the **BIG** game!*

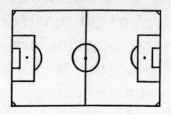

1 Summer Soccer

'Can't wait for school to start again next week.'

Christopher Weston propped himself up on his elbow in alarm. Never before had he heard his elder brother, Andrew, say that he was actually wanting to go to school.

'Are you feeling all right?' he asked, wiggling a finger in his ear as if to clear any blockage.

Andrew grinned at him. 'Don't worry, I haven't got sunstroke or anything. I've been looking forward to the new term ever since we got back from the Cubs' summer camp.'

'Why?'

'Soccer season begins of course.'

'Oh, is that all? Might have guessed.'

'What do you mean, *is that all*?"' Andrew mocked. 'I'm going to be in the school team at last. What else is more important than that?'

Chris could have named several things, but knew it wasn't worth the effort. All Andrew had wanted to do, right through the holidays, was play football. Even today, in the middle of

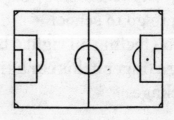

a hot afternoon, he had insisted on them having yet another kickabout in the back garden.

But now both boys were sprawled out on the lawn, stripped to the waist, taking a breather from the game in their home-made, wooden goal. They had built it themselves only days before.

'Think you stand a chance of being captain?' Chris asked instead.

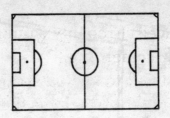

Andrew sighed and sat up. 'Nah, don't suppose so. Old Jonesy's almost bound to pick Tim Lawrence. There's only him and Duggie left from last year's team and Tim's the best player.'

'Even better than you?' Chris teased.

'Watch it! Best out of them two, I meant.'

'So why didn't the headmaster put you in the team last year too, if you're so good?' said Chris, unable to resist a further taunt, despite the risk of making Andrew mad.

'Because, little brother,' he said slowly, giving him a long, hard stare, 'me and Mr Jones don't always get on all that well. Probably thinks I'm too cheeky or something.'

Chris tried to keep a straight face, not wishing to stretch his luck too far. 'He'll need you this season, though, won't he?'

'Course he will. Got no defence, have they, without me.'

Any further boasting was stopped by a frothing mass of fur as a black-and-white collie suddenly bounded up, bent on licking his face.

'Get off, Shoot, will you!' Andrew yelled, pushing the dog away. 'I had a wash last week.'

'Here, boy,' urged Chris, patting his side. 'You can come and fan me with your tail!'

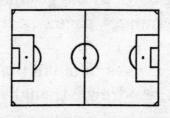

Their mother called to them from the house. 'Take Shoot for a walk, please, boys, I'm busy.'

'Aw, Mum, so are we,' Andrew grumbled. 'We're practising for the new season.'

'Doesn't look much like it to me,' she laughed. 'The dog needs some real exercise, even if you two don't.'

It was no use arguing with Mum. As she threw the lead out to them, Andrew jumped to his feet and blasted the ball at the goal in a flash of temper.

The shot smacked against the far post with a force that was more than the rickety frame could stand. The upright creaked in protest and tilted backwards, sending the crossbar crashing down to the ground.

The brothers gazed sadly at the wreckage.

'Took us ages to make that an' all,' groaned Andrew, though secretly

quite proud of the damage his power-drive had caused. 'Have to use longer nails next time.'

Chris shrugged, looking at it from a goalkeeper's point of view, his own favourite position. 'Could have been worse, I guess.'

'Oh yeah? Tell me how.'

'I might have been underneath it at the time . . .'

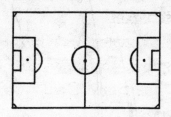

2 Hot Dog

Andrew dribbled the football along the quiet village lane towards the recreation ground, his younger brother left trailing behind with Shoot.

Several lads from Andrew's class at Danebridge Primary School, most of them two years older than Chris, were already there playing cricket.

'C'mon, you lot, put those stumps away,' he greeted them, hoofing the

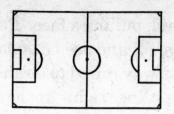

ball up into the air to make it land right in the middle of their pitch. 'It's the soccer season again now.'

John Duggan didn't need much persuading to swap sports. There was nothing he loved better than scoring goals. 'Yeah, let's have some shooting practice.'

'Good idea, our kid can go in goal for us,' Andrew said as Chris arrived.

'No way,' Simon Garner protested. 'I'm going to be school team goalie this year. I need some practice.'

'Little Westy can be behind the goal, fetching everything that big brother slices wide,' Duggie scoffed.

'I'm not just being your ball boy,'

Chris said, pulling a face. 'Besides, I'd rather go off and see Grandad.'

On his way round to Grandad's cottage, nestling right up against the recky, Chris let Shoot run free along the bank of the river Dane. He threw a few sticks for the dog to chase and twice Shoot ended up in the water, emerging to shake himself all over his young master.

Upset at first to be left out of the game, Shoot's antics soon had Chris smiling again. And his smile turned into a mischievous grin when he peered over the back garden wall of the cottage.

Grandad was asleep in an old canvas deckchair, pipe in his lap and the lawn mower standing idle on the partly-cut grass. Somehow he seemed to sense he was being watched and his eyes flickered reluctantly open.

'Sorry to disturb you, Grandad, I

can see you're busy gardening,' Chris smirked. 'Fancy a hot dog?'

'What, in this weather?' Grandad wheezed. 'You must be joking.'

'No, I'm not – here it is.'

A panting Shoot bolted through the gate to frisk around the chair, tongue lolling out of one side of his mouth.

Grandad pushed the dog playfully away as he eased himself to his feet.

'You keep them wet paws to yourself, you little pest, and that wet tongue. He's been in the river again, hasn't he?'

'Got to try and cool off somehow,' Chris said.

'Looks like you've got the right idea too, not galloping around like Andrew and the rest I can see over there.'

Chris frowned. 'They don't want me. I'm too young.'

Grandad shook his head and put his hand on the boy's bare shoulder. 'Look, it's not how old you are that matters, it's how good you are. Leave Shoot here with me for a bit and you go back and show 'em who's the real number one goalkeeper round this place!'

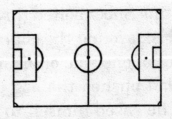

'Goal!' screamed Duggie. 'Beat you all ends up, Simon.'

'Lucky,' his friend replied. 'Had it covered till it hit a bump.'

'Our kid would have saved it,' Andrew said as Chris jogged off to fetch the ball from the undergrowth beyond the pitch.

'Come off it! If Simon couldn't, nobody could.'

'Want a bet? You wait till you see Chris in action soon for the Cubs.'

Tim Lawrence joined in. 'You two talking about the Soccer Sixes? My pack's going to win that easy.'

'Not if I can help it,' Andrew laughed. He and Tim were leading members of the two rival Cub packs in Danebridge, both hoping for success in the annual area tournament in the nearby town of Selworth.

'All my men will be in the school

23

team as well this year, including Duggie and Simon here,' Tim pointed out. 'Who can stop us?'

'Me and Chris for a start. We've been practising a lot in the garden. He's getting really good in goal.'

'You're a defender – your shooting would make anybody look good,' Duggie joked, making sure he kept out of Andrew's reach as he said it.

Simon booted the ball back into play to put an end to any argument and Tim laid it perfectly into Duggie's path. The striker hit it in his stride with great power, taking the keeper by surprise.

The ball flashed past him just under the crossbar, but Chris behind the goal had more time to react. He dived high to his right and clung on to the ball in mid air at full stretch in spectacular fashion.

'Well caught!' Tim cried out. 'Saved yourself a long chase.'

Chris's catch won him the chance to go in goal properly after a while, where he impressed them several times with his clean handling of the ball. Simon tried not to look too worried.

'Takes after Grandad,' Andrew said.

'What do you mean?' asked Tim.

'Grandad used to play in goal for the village team right here on this pitch. Best keeper they ever had.'

'How do you know?' Duggie sneered. 'Ever see him play?'

'Don't be stupid, course not, but loads of people have told me. He's always giving Chris tips about goal-keeping.'

'Perhaps Simon will have to watch out,' Tim smiled. 'If he starts letting in a few goals, Mr Jones might be tempted to pick your Chris instead.'

'Or even your grandad!' cackled Duggie.

Andrew retold the tale later when he and Chris collected Shoot. 'It's not just me Christopher takes after,' Grandad reminded them. 'Your dad often played in goal, too.'

The brothers looked at each other. Dad was rarely mentioned at home now, ever since he had suddenly disappeared two years ago and went to live abroad. They hadn't seen him again.

Andrew broke the awkward silence. 'Guess that goalies kind of run in our family, then, don't they?'

'Not in this heat, they don't,' Grandad chuckled. 'These days, I'm afraid, this old goalie walks!'

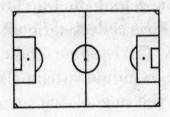

3 Six-pack

'Knew it would be you.'

The headmaster's decision to name Tim as school soccer captain came as no surprise, but Andrew still had to hide his own disappointment.

'No hard feelings, I hope,' Tim replied, realizing how much his friend had wanted the honour himself.

Andrew shook his head. 'Course not. Guess you deserve it really.'

Mr Jones had waited until halfway through the main trial game on the recky before announcing the expected news, then reshuffled the sides for the second half. Andrew and Tim now found themselves in the same team and, like everyone else, soon twigged what the headmaster was up to!

It was clear that he had put his best eleven players together to see how they shaped up. Their confidence boosted, Tim's 'A' team began to play like champions already, passing the ball around between them well and moving quickly into spaces. They all wanted it back again to show what they could do and prove that Mr Jones had made the right choice.

As for Chris, now in the 'B' team goal, he saw rather more of the ball than he might have wished. The stronger opponents swarmed around his penalty area in one attack after another, keeping him too busy to feel nervous or worry about any mistakes that he made.

He was lucky enough to get away with one fumble when an attacker somehow poked the dropped ball wide, but his next slip was more costly.

It was his own brother, too, who started the move which led to Chris's embarrassment. Andrew won the ball with a firm tackle on the halfway line, looked up and aimed a pass ahead of Tim as the captain cut in from the left touchline towards the penalty area.

Chris thought he could reach the ball first and dashed off his goal-line, but Tim was too swift for him. The young keeper was stranded out of position as the ball was whipped away from his wild lunge and stroked across to Duggie.

The unmarked striker showed no mercy. He fired his shot dead straight

through the open goal and with no net to catch it, the ball sped on and buried itself in the long grass under the trees. Chris knew the trudge to the undergrowth well, but he could have done without Duggie's stinging taunt. 'Better go and ask your old grandad for some more tips, little Westy!'

Although beaten four times in the end, Chris did at least produce a few good saves too. His best moment, by far, came late in the game when he dived low to his left to smother an effort from Andrew.

'Well stopped, our kid,' Andrew praised his brother, taking his mates' teasing in good spirit. 'We'll have some more like that from you in the Sixes.'

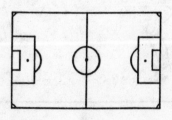

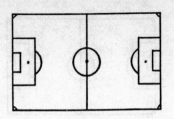

'Right!' said Akela before the start of the first group game. 'Go out and show people how you can play. Enjoy it, that's the main thing.'

The pack leader and football coach of the 1st Danebridge Cubs' team turned to Andrew, his captain. 'I'm relying on you to help the younger lads. Keep encouraging them.'

'I will, Akela,' Andrew replied, taking the job seriously. He would be leaving the Cubs soon to join the Scouts and was wanting to skipper his pack to victory in the tournament to finish on a high note.

The talents and ages of the players from the many packs in the Selworth area varied widely. Some were already

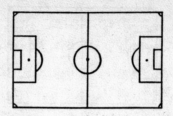

experienced footballers for their school teams, some were still too young and some, in truth, were not really good enough to be chosen yet.

But now, on a warm, sunny, September afternoon, they had their chance to take part in a big soccer tournament. They were all raring to go and do their best for the Cubs.

Andrew's team, however, got off to a bad start. Playing against a pack from Selworth itself, they were a goal down before Chris had even touched the ball.

An Asian lad, slimly built and very quick, zipped round a defender's rather nervous challenge and slid the ball past Chris from just outside the goalkeeper's semi-circular area.

'C'mon!' Andrew cried out in frustration. 'What kind of a tackle d'you call that?'

Then he caught Akela's eye and remembered his promise. 'OK, don't worry about it. That kid's so fast, just try and mark him tighter from now on, right?'

The boy nodded, feeling a little better, but he needed Andrew to come to his rescue several times more as he struggled to cope with the speed of the attacker called Rakesh. It was mostly due to the captain that there was no further scoring in the short match, but

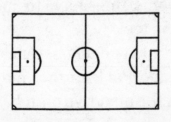

a marvellous double save from Chris near the end prevented a heavier defeat.

First he parried an awkward skidding drive and then, as the ball rebounded outside the area, it was Rakesh who pounced on it before anyone else. He could hardly believe it when the goalkeeper recovered in time to block his shot as well and scoop the ball over the crossbar.

'How did you keep that one out?' Rakesh grinned, entering the area to help him up. 'Dead cert second goal that was.'

'Just hit my legs,' Chris admitted modestly. But as Grandad had often told him, he knew that even the best goalies sometimes have to make saves with their feet.

Despite this early setback, the 1st Danebridge Pack in fact managed to win both the next two matches against

weaker sides and qualify for the quarter-finals as runners-up in their group.

Mr Jones arrived on the scene at this stage in the hope of watching many of his own soccer squad in action, just in time to see Chris play a blinder.

'Promising young keeper, your grandson,' he said to Grandad after a fierce volley was pushed to safety round a post.

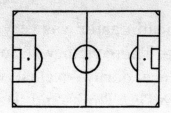

Grandad had helped to transport the Cubs to the tournament, ready as always to support Andrew and Chris in their sporting activities in any way that he could. 'Aye, that's true,' he nodded proudly. 'You haven't got a better goalie in your school from what I've seen.'

Mr Jones smiled. 'His chance will come one day, that's for sure.'

Chris helped that future day come a little closer with a whole series of excellent saves, keeping a clean sheet for the first time in the competition. And to complete a fine family double act, Andrew scored the only goal of the game, his third altogether, which put them through to the semi-finals.

The headmaster was very glad that he came. Their victory set up a fascinating local derby – a clash with their great rivals, Tim's 2nd Danebridge Pack!

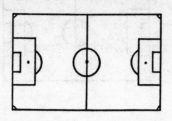

4 *Do Your Best*

'Good luck, everyone,' Akela called out to both the Danebridge packs before the kick-off. 'May the best team win.'

'Yeah – as long as it's us,' Andrew added under his breath, certain that Tim would be thinking exactly the same thing.

Beating their friends would in many ways be more important than winning the actual tournament itself.

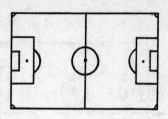

Each pack's pride was at stake. All the pre-match joking and mickey-taking between the players would be nothing, they feared, compared to what the losers might have to suffer afterwards from their cocky conquerors.

Most of Duggie's jibes were aimed at Chris in an attempt to put him off. 'Well, look who it is – our little ball boy again!'

Chris flushed, but tried to give back as good as he got. 'This time I'll be saving your shots in front of the goal, not behind it.'

Duggie wasted no time in testing him out, too, when the game began. He hit a shot from the wing which slithered along the ground, bang on target, but the goalkeeper was equal to it.

He made sure his body was right behind his hands, as Grandad always insisted when they practised together, and it was a good job that he did so. The ball bobbled through his grasp but thudded against his chest, and he was able to dive on to it again before it escaped from the area.

At the other end, Simon proved just as safe and the two goalies kept the scoresheet blank at half-time. Straight after the change-round, however, Andrew, of all people, missed a clear chance to put his team ahead.

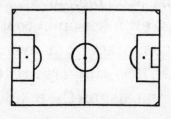

With only Simon to beat, he blazed the
ball wildly over the bar when a care-
ful, accurate side-footer was all that
was needed to score.

Sadly, instead of being a goal up,
they were soon one down. Tim was to
give Andrew a lesson in cool finishing
from close range, but even his shot
brushed Chris's fingers first on its way
in, glancing also off the inside of a post.

Andrew decided to stay up in attack now to try and snatch an equalizer, but it was a gamble that didn't pay off. His absence from defence left a large hole which Duggie soon used to his own benefit.

Receiving a pass from Tim, he found himself in so much space, he had time to give the young goalkeeper a triumphant grin before hammering the ball past him. Chris's only consolation was that at least there was a net this time to save him another long trek.

At the final whistle, Andrew was big enough to go up and shake Tim's hand and wish him luck, but the 2-0 defeat hurt him badly.

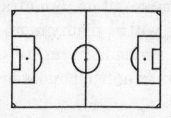

'Never mind, Andrew, you can't win 'em all,' Grandad said as the brothers joined him on the touchline to watch the Final. 'This is one big game you'll have to miss out on, I'm afraid.'

'There will be plenty more to come,' Andrew replied, trying to cover his disappointment. 'I'll make sure of that all right!'

Tim's 2nd Danebridge Cubs' Pack believed that the Cup was as good as in the trophy cabinet in their village hut. Nothing could stand in their way now – apart from the 9th Selworth outfit and Rakesh.

It was the winger's pace which took them by surprise, just as it had Andrew's side earlier in the tournament. Rakesh was allowed to run free down the right touchline and his cross was tucked neatly past Simon into the corner of the goal by the Selworth captain.

'Perhaps we should have warned them about that lad,' Akela smiled.

'He sure needs special marking,' said Andrew. 'Give him too much room

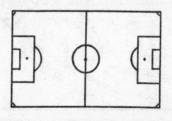

and he'll take any defence apart.'

As if to prove his words, Rakesh sped clear again but his shot on the run clipped the woodwork. It was the only piece of luck that Tim's team enjoyed. For once, Duggie seemed to have completely lost his magic touch and chance after chance at the other end went begging.

Usually the deadliest of strikers, he sliced one shot so far wide, the ball hit the corner flag instead of the goal, and then poked another tame effort straight at the keeper. Not even the captain could find his true form and inspire his pack to victory, missing an open goal himself.

They ended up losing 1-0 and both Tim and Andrew had to look on enviously as the Selworth captain lifted the Sixes Cup to great cheers.

'If we could have fielded a joint

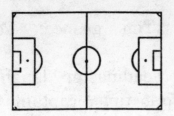

Danebridge team, they wouldn't have beaten us, I know,' sighed Tim.

'Yeah, that's right,' Andrew agreed. 'Six or eleven-a-side, they'd have no chance against us at full strength.'

'We'd slaughter 'em!' put in Duggie.

Mr Jones had come up behind them unnoticed. 'Well played, boys,' he began, making them jump, and they whirled round to face him. 'Glad to hear you'd all love another crack at them. It so happens I've just fixed up our first league match – and guess who we've got?'

They followed his eyes towards the grinning group of Selworth boys, holding up their medals for the photographs in the sunshine.

'No!' Tim gasped. 'You don't mean . . .'

The headmaster laughed. 'Yes, right first time, captain. Selworth School at home, ten o'clock kick-off next Saturday morning!'

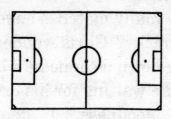

5 Debut Day

'You will be watching, won't you, Grandad?'

Andrew had dashed straight to the cottage after the final practice session for the Selworth game, almost bursting with excitement. He had been picked to play at centre-back, right at the heart of the defence.

'Course I will,' Grandad reassured him. 'I'll be here, as always, leaning on my old garden wall – my own little grandstand view.'

'How many matches have you seen on the recky?' Chris wondered aloud, putting down a comic he'd been reading while waiting for his brother.

'Oh, goodness, I don't know,' Grandad laughed. 'Hundreds and hundreds, must be, and thousands of players – good and bad.'

'Anybody famous?' Andrew asked keenly.

Grandad smoothed down his moustache in thought, his eyes twinkling. 'Well, not as a footballer, as far as I can recall. Mind you, we did have a bank robber once! Got arrested after scoring a hat-trick . . .'

'You're making that up,' Andrew cried. 'C'mon, Grandad, I'm being serious. If nobody from our village has ever become a professional footballer, my ambition is to be the first!'

'Well, every future soccer star's got to start their career somewhere,' Grandad said, sensing the boy's determination. 'And I guess Danebridge recky is as good a place as any.'

Chris butted in again. 'I just want to play in goal for Danebridge like you did, Grandad – and Dad, as well, of course.'

Grandad was delighted. 'And I've

still got an ambition left, too, y'know – even at my age.'

'What's that?' they chorused.

'Well, now that you're both getting old enough, I'm looking forward to seeing the two of you play together here for the school team.'

Chris gave a little groan. 'Sorry, Grandad, you might have to wait a while yet. By the time I get chosen, Andrew will have left.'

The old man smiled and nudged Chris gently on the arm with his elbow. 'Doubt it. From what I've seen, reckon you'll be wearing that goalkeeper's green jersey sooner than you think.'

Andrew tried to steer the talk back on to his own debut, never mind his kid brother's. 'We're after revenge on Saturday – now it's a proper eleven-a-side match, we're going to show 'em who's boss.'

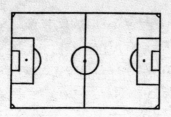

'Maybe, but just don't go building up your hopes too much,' Grandad said wisely, starting to light his curved pipe. 'It's a funny old game, football. And I should know, I've seen it all – anything can happen . . .'

'That Rakesh is only one of their subs,' Andrew gasped, spotting the Asian lad still in his tracksuit top among Selworth's light-blue kit.

Simon broke off from their pre-match practice to stand and stare. 'You're right. Good news, that is, I'd been dreading facing him again.'

'Bad news, I'd say,' Andrew reckoned. 'They must be better than we

thought, if they can afford to leave out someone like him.'

The defender rolled up the sleeves of his red and white striped shirt, so thrilled to be wearing the Danebridge colours for the first time. 'Anyway, I don't care who's playing, I'm ready for 'em,' he stated boldly. 'Let's get kicked off.'

As the Danebridge and Selworth

teams lined up on a bright, autumn morning, Chris was already in action, keeping goal between two sports bags in a kickabout game with several friends near the main pitch. As he swooped on to a low shot before it could sneak through, he recognized a voice behind him.

'Can I join in? I get fed up just hanging around, watching.'

Chris stood up, still holding on to

the ball. 'I remember you from the Cubs' Sixes,' he said shyly.

'I haven't forgotten you either,' Rakesh replied. 'You stopped us scoring a few more goals with saves like that.'

'You were brill,' Chris said, returning the compliment. 'Why aren't you playing today?'

'Only got picked as sub,' he explained with a shrug. 'The others are all a year older than me.'

'I know how you feel,' Chris sighed. 'Even my big brother's had to wait till now to make his debut for the school.'

Rakesh grinned as Andrew was pointed out. 'Oh, it's him, is it? I've still got the bruises to show for his tackling last week! Tried to slow me down a bit.'

Chris laughed. 'Well he didn't succeed.'

'No, and I hope to prove that to him myself later. Teacher's said I'll be on

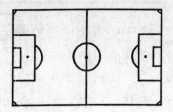

after half-time so I want to be nicely warmed up by then.'

Their game re-started with Rakesh but before he'd even had a kick, a cheer went up and they all glanced round. Too late! The Danebridge players were already celebrating Duggie's first goal of the season.

The younger lads missed seeing his second as well. But by that time, Rakesh had also scored two of his own, making Chris regret his daft decision to let him play for the other side in their kickabout game.

The Selworth keeper was none too happy either. He had been at fault with the opening goal and just when he'd thought the striker's next shot

was going way over the bar, the ball dipped down late and flew in just beneath the high crossbar. Duggie knew the size of the big goals on the recky pitch far better than he did.

'Fantastic!' whooped Andrew after he'd raced up and slapped Duggie's raised hand in delight. 'Maybe this is going to be dead easy after all.'

'Long way to go yet,' Tim warned

him. 'You just make sure they don't score any.'

As Andrew took up his position again in defence, he realized somebody else was also trying to tell him to calm down. The signals from the garden wall served to remind him of one of Grandad's favourite sayings.

'A game's never won until the referee blows the final whistle.'

And before this match was over, all the players were going to learn that important soccer lesson . . .

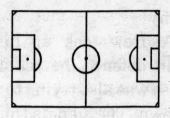

6 Great Game

Andrew was furious. With himself and with the other defenders.

'C'mon, that was a sloppy goal to give away,' he yelled as Simon miserably fished the ball out the back of the net.

Nor was their captain best pleased with his team's poor marking at a corner, allowing the Selworth player far too much freedom to control the ball and shoot.

'Told you all to watch out,' Tim said crossly. 'Now we've gone and let them back in the game.'

As Tim feared, the goal perked the visitors up and they were on top for the rest of the first half. Andrew worked like a beaver to prevent the defensive dam bursting under the pressure of a flood of attacks and pulled off an amazing escape act just before the interval.

The equalizer looked certain when Simon was caught out of his goal and the ball was lobbed over his head. Everyone, it seemed, stopped and gave up to watch it bouncing towards the welcoming net – but not Andrew.

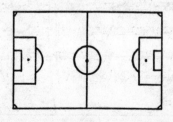

Hoping against hope, he simply kept chasing, desperate to reach the ball before it crossed the line. And he did – just! With less than a metre to spare, Andrew somehow managed to hook the ball away, tumbling head over heels into the goal himself instead.

He was so tangled up in the netting, trapped by his studs like a helpless fly in a giant spider's web, that play had to be halted while the referee went to his rescue. Andrew emerged red-faced, but grinning, to loud applause from the spectators.

'You're a better goal-hanger than me,' Duggie joked as they gathered round Mr Jones for the half-time pep talk.

Chris joined them, his own game now abandoned. 'What were you doing dangling upside-down in the goal?' he asked when the group broke up.

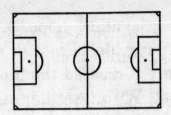

Andrew was stunned, unable to believe that his brother had missed his best moment. 'What a stupid question! You mean you didn't see my brilliant clearance off the line?'

Chris shook his head. 'Sorry. When I looked round to check what the cheering was about, all I could see was you doing a headstand.'

Andrew felt like hitting him. 'Typical! Sunbathing, were you?'

'I was playing football with Rakesh actually,' Chris defended himself. 'He's on great form – we just couldn't stop him scoring.'

'I'll deal with him all right,' Andrew boasted. 'You watch.'

'Oh, I will,' Chris said cheekily. 'I'm not going to miss this!'

Even Grandad had come for a closer look at the second half, appearing on the touchline with Shoot lying at his side. 'Well played,' he called to Andrew. 'Keep it up, don't relax.'

There was no chance for anybody to do that, especially with Rakesh now sent on, as promised, to bomb down the right wing. The left back couldn't match such explosive pace and Andrew had to cover across twice in the first few minutes to help him out.

But not even Andrew could stop the winger for long from levelling the

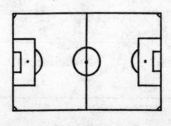

scores. Rakesh outsprinted everybody to race clear for goal and then fooled Simon with a last-second body swerve, dribbling the ball past him before tapping it into the empty goal.

Andrew stood dejected, hands on hips, shaking his head at how they had thrown away a two-goal lead. He glared at Rakesh's little dance of celebration. 'Well you won't be doing that again,' he said under his breath. 'Not if I can do anything about it.'

Five minutes later, Andrew was as good as his word, but not quite in the way that he'd intended. Seeing Rakesh this time cut inside from the wing, hurtling for goal with the ball under the close control of his flying feet, Andrew homed in across his path like a torpedo.

Rakesh sensed the danger and increased his speed even more, the extra burst taking him into the

penalty area. Just as he steadied himself a fraction for the shot, however,
the defender struck. Andrew
stretched out a long leg to nudge the
ball away – but didn't quite make it.
His boot caught Rakesh instead,
knocking him off-balance and sending
him sprawling to the ground.

'Penalty!'

Andrew, down on his knees, held up
his hands in horror and then clamped
them to his ears as if to deafen the
appeals.

And to make matters worse, as the
referee pointed to the penalty spot,
there was a pitch invasion. Two boys
tried to stop the intruder, but the first
Andrew knew about it was when his
face was licked.

Shoot had been startled by the sud-
den loud shouts and leapt up, jerking
the lead from Grandad's loose grip.
Seeing Andrew nearby, he ran to him

72

in greeting, barking with excitement,
but soon realized his master was in no
mood to play. His tail disappeared
between his legs.

'Get him off!' Andrew snarled as
Chris came on to grab the trailing
lead. 'Suppose you saw what hap-
pened that time OK, didn't you?'

"Fraid so, but don't get mad at
Shoot,' Chris said, tugging the dog

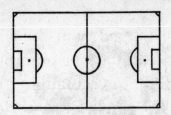

away. 'He might be the only friend you've got if this penalty costs us the match!'

Andrew stood on the edge of the area with all the other players to watch the duel between goalkeeper and penalty-taker, praying that Simon might yet save him. As the Selworth captain made contact, Simon dived to his right, but the ball flew dead straight. If the keeper had stayed where he was, it would have hit him smack in the stomach.

'Forget about it, Andrew,' Grandad called out as Danebridge now found themselves 2-3 down. 'Just get on with the game.'

'Your grandad's right,' added Tim.

74

'Can't be helped, you did your best. About the only other one round here who could have caught up with Rakesh like that was your dog.'

'Yeah, and I bet he would have tripped him up too!' grunted Duggie.

Andrew tried to look on the bright side again. 'C'mon, team, we can still do it,' he shouted to urge them all on. 'There's still time.'

But when he saw the referee carefully studying his watch, Andrew knew there could not really be much longer left. Determined to make up for his mistake, he went into the next tackle on Rakesh just as strongly as ever and this time won the ball cleanly. Moving it on to Tim, Andrew kept charging forward, adding his own weight to the attack as well.

The powerful defender strode deep into the Selworth half, demanding the ball back again. When it came,

Andrew hit it first time, hard and low towards goal, but he was out of luck. An opponent managed to get his body in the way and deflect the shot wide.

Andrew decided to stay up for the left-wing corner, hoping for a possible header at goal himself. Both he and Duggie lurked by the far post as Tim curled the ball high and long towards them with the inside of his right boot – but neither of Tim's intended targets could reach it.

Nor could the goalkeeper. The ball swung over everybody's heads and swirled into the top corner of the net, untouched.

'Fluke!' yelled Duggie into Tim's ear as the captain was half-suffocated under the crush of his jubilant team-mates.

'Who cares?' Tim choked back. 'They all count.'

To the relief of two exhausted sides,

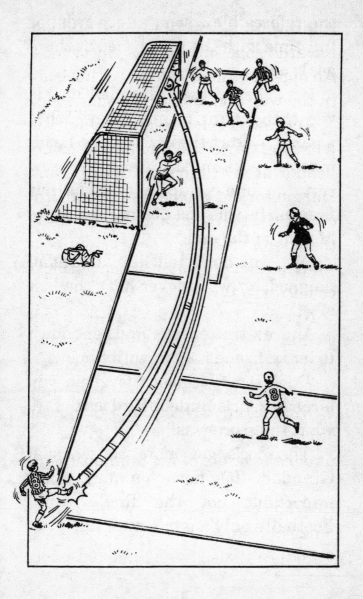

the referee blew soon afterwards for full-time with the match tied at three goals each.

Mr Jones passed Grandad on his way to the changing hut. 'Phew! What a game to start the season!' the head-master exclaimed. 'Your Andrew certainly had his ups and downs, but I reckon he was just about *"Man of the Match"* in the end.'

'Aye, but don't tell him,' Grandad laughed, 'or we'll never hear the last of it!'

Andrew trotted over and bent down to make friends again with Shoot.

'Don't worry, Shoot's forgiven you already,' Chris smiled. 'He doesn't care what the score was!'

'The dog's got more sense,' said Grandad. 'It's how you play that's important, not the final result. Football's only a game after all.'

'But it's a great game,' Andrew enthused. 'The best in the world!'

Grandad chuckled. 'Even if you lose?'

Andrew hesitated only for a moment. 'Win or lose,' he said firmly.

'Or draw,' added Chris, giving Shoot an extra little pat.

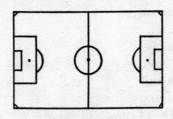

THE END

L.

A SELECTED LIST OF TITLES
AVAILABLE FROM YOUNG CORGI BOOKS

THE PRICES SHOWN BELOW WERE CORRECT AT THE TIME OF GOING
TO PRESS. HOWEVER TRANSWORLD PUBLISHERS RESERVE THE
RIGHT TO SHOW NEW PRICES ON COVERS WHICH MAY DIFFER FROM
THOSE PREVIOUSLY ADVERTISED IN THE TEXT OR ELSEWHERE.

☐ 0 552 52713 0	**ROYAL BLUNDER**	*Henrietta Branford*	£2.50
☐ 0 552 52759 9	**ROYAL BLUNDER AND THE HAUNTED HOUSE**	*Henrietta Branford*	£2.50
☐ 0 552 52824 2	**THE BIG CHANCE**	*Rob Childs*	£2.99
☐ 0 552 52581 2	**THE BIG DAY**	*Rob Childs*	£2.50
☐ 0 552 54297 0	**THE BIG FOOTBALL COLLECTION OMNIBUS**	*Rob Childs*	£3.99
☐ 0 552 52804 8	**THE BIG GAME**	*Rob Childs*	£2.99
☐ 0 552 52760 2	**THE BIG GOAL**	*Rob Childs*	£2.50
☐ 0 552 52662 2	**THE BIG HIT**	*Rob Childs*	£2.50
☐ 0 552 52663 0	**THE BIG KICK**	*Rob Childs*	£2.99
☐ 0 552 52451 4	**THE BIG MATCH**	*Rob Childs*	£2.50
☐ 0 552 52823 4	**THE BIG PRIZE**	*Rob Childs*	£2.50
☐ 0 552 52825 0	**THE BIG STAR**	*Rob Childs*	£2.50
☐ 0 552 52747 5	**HENRIETTA AND THE GHOST CHASE**	*Stan Cullimore*	£2.50
☐ 0 552 52829 3	**HENRIETTA AND THE MAGIC TRICK**	*Stan Cullimore*	£2.50
☐ 0 552 52828 5	**HENRIETTA'S POCKET MONEY**	*Stan Cullimore*	£2.50
☐ 0 552 52749 1	**THE OLDEST SNOWMAN IN THE WORLD**	*Eric Johns*	£2.50
☐ 0 552 52802 1	**COUNT BORIS AND THE MIDSUMMER MADNESS**	*Ann Jungman*	£2.50
☐ 0 552 52795 5	**CONNIE AND ROLLO**	*Dick King-Smith*	£2.50
☐ 0 552 52523 5	**ESP**	*Dick King-Smith*	£2.99
☐ 0 552 52731 9	**THE GUARD DOG**	*Dick King-Smith*	£2.50
☐ 0 552 14215 8	**THE GUARD DOG (Book and Tape)**	*Dick King-Smith*	£4.99
☐ 0 552 52785 8	**HORSE PIE**	*Dick King-Smith*	£2.50
☐ 0 552 52831 5	**HORSE PIE (Book and Tape)**	*Dick King-Smith*	£4.99
☐ 0 552 20413 7	**JUNGLE JINGLES (Audio)**	*Dick King-Smith*	£3.49
☐ 0 552 52664 9	**CALCULATOR ANNIE**	*Alexander McCall Smith*	£2.50
☐ 0 552 52476 X	**MIKE'S MAGIC SEEDS**	*Alexander McCall Smith*	£2.50
☐ 0 552 52803 X	**TEACHER TROUBLE**	*Alexander McCall Smith*	£2.99